GHOST MAGNET

CRIME AND MAGIC IN THE NEW RUSSIA # 1

JAMES BEACH

MIND
FU

GHOST MAGNET

This is a work of fiction. All the characters and events portrayed, except for purposes of satire, are fictional and any resemblance to real people or incidents is purely coincidental.

A Mind Fu original book. 29 Grove St., #340 San Francisco, CA 94102

ISBN: 978-1-945451-04-1

Cover design by James Beach

First printing. May 2018

VI.2

The fading evening light glinted off the dying eyes of drug addicts, in a large and formerly beautiful house in the Sestoretsk district outlying St. Petersburg. The only sober man inside wondered how in hell he'd come to this.

Looking into his past, Aurelian Vyzhivshiy saw little fortune and none of it good. St. Petersburg had quickly given him a choice - steal or starve. He had become a thief, and a good one. Yet his rewards never seemed to match up with his efforts. The last of several scores, a robbery of antique gems from the State Hermitage Museum, had gone so wrong that he only barely escaped.

Now instead of being drunk in a fine hotel like a winning gambler, he hid here in a drug den. His acquaintance Pavel was letting him stay here, for a price – enough rubles for Pavel to get more of a new drug called Prizrak. It was said to be similar to Kokodril, so named because it had turned men's skins scaly like a crocodile before it killed them. Prizrak was simpler and more unsettling, as it seemed to make men rot from inside until they moved like wraiths. The drug had to bring some fantastic kind of high. Once someone got on it, they stayed on it for the rest of their shortened lives.

Aurelian had known Pavel when he'd first come to St. Petersburg, years ago. He had wanted to do gigantic things once. Now all he wanted was this high. He described it as like seeing memories he couldn't know, and feeling his own flesh like a stranger. He'd offered Aurelian a taste of the drug himself. Aurelian had rarely declined an offer faster.

The door downstairs opened, and cold fresh outside air blew in. Like any thief who made it to adulthood, he became fully alert. He leaned forward to see who entered. His heart calmed on seeing they were clearly not police, but private citizens – a thin man in his late 50s wearing an immaculate business suit, followed by three larger, younger men in cheap suits.

Those pathetic denizens lying on the floor who were still conscious moved weakly and wearily out of their way like dying and polluted rivers before Moses.

From the railing above, Aurelian watched with hooded eyes. Even though they were not police, their arrival was unsettling. They were all too healthy to be here for the drugs. The younger men all looked big. One was slim and seemed like a viper, another was of a medium size that would easily be ignored in a crowd. The third one who stood closest to the older man had a shaven head, and he looked even bigger than the others. Aurelian decided all three of them must be bodyguards, as they moved with the physical confidence of those used to winning fights.

The older man looked around, and barked an order. The largest of his apparent bodyguards, a shaven-headed hulk of a man, reached down and picked up a particular junkie. They began to ask the addict questions.

Aurelian couldn't hear the conversation, but the fact it was even happening at all was a sign of nothing good. He moved back from the railing and turned to a man seated on the floor, busy staring at nothing with his mind in numbing dreams.

"Pavel!" Aurelian whispered.

The man kept staring.

"Hey!" Aurelian whispered louder, risking alerting others to his presence. Pavel started, and regarded him with glazed and disapproving eyes.

"Who is that?" Aurelian whispered, and pointed to the group who'd just entered.

Pavel leaned forward with strange difficulty, and

squinted. "That is Coba," he whispered back. "Mikhail Coba. This is his place."

Aurelian scowled. He had heard of the man. This was no good at all. Mikhail Coba had been a coroner for years, known among the underworld as a man who could make any death look accidental for a fee. Then his wife and children died. He retired from his official job, and found a new career that was entirely illegal - making inconvenient corpses disappear. He showed a legendary effectiveness in this useful service, and had carved out a niche business for St. Petersburg's most brutal crime groups. Grudging respect as a quiet and reliable player allowed him to develop a side business of selling drugs. It made sense that he would create his own lodging house for addicts—not out of sympathy, but out of convenience. A place for customers to use the goods that slowly killed them, until their flesh gave out and it was time to make their dead husks disappear.

None of which was Aurelian's business. This was only supposed to be a convenient spot to avoid the long reach and cold grip of the St. Petersburg police. "You didn't say this was his place!"

"But it is." Pavel nodded at the wisdom of this, leaned back, and returned to the surcease of the drug.

Aurelian cursed under his breath. He had passage on a freighter to Odessa just before dawn. Helsinki was only a few hours' drive from St. Petersburg, while Odessa would take days by boat. But Helsinki was in the EU and would demand to see his papers. Odessa was in Ukraine, and was from all he'd heard a far easier place to get some fake papers and a new start.

He had heard that the criminal world in Odessa was in some ways even more capricious and violent than St. Petersburg's, and the rest of Ukraine had less work for his current set of skills. Even so, there were not yet police looking for him in Odessa.

Getting that passage had cost nearly all his hard-stolen money. He had given the remainder to Pavel in exchange for hiding here. All he needed was a simple and uncomplicated place to stay before he headed to the shipyards, and his junkie friend had led him to a drug lord's house. A man who was now going through the house and asking questions of people.

"Why is he asking them questions?" Aurelian whispered. With herculean effort, Pavel mustered enough energy to shrug. "Give me back my money!" Aurelian hissed.

"It's in my arm," Pavel giggled. "It is so good...you must try it."

Aurelian got up to a low crouch and picked up his back-pack, with all his remaining possessions in the world. He watched as Coba made his way across the downstairs room, occasionally leaning down to talk to a junkie and then moving forward. Aurelian cursed further as he saw they were heading to the stairs. He stayed in a crouch as he slowly moved away from the top of the stairs. He acciden-tally stepped on someone's hand, only noticing this on hearing a low moan from a nearly comatose former workman lying in his own filth. Aurelian murmured a reflexive apology, realizing while saying it that the man was unlikely to even hear him. If he were a colder man he'd rob the pathetic bastard of what little he had left before he ran out of this place. He sighed. He never was smart.

He looked in the only open room off the landing, and cursed again. The room had no windows to escape through.

He made it around a corner, successfully out of sight. Mikhail Coba and his crew were halfway up the stairs by the sound of it. He heard an older voice say "That one." Aurelian realized that must be Coba. The man spoke in a flat, clipped Georgian accent. Aurelian liked this even less, if that were possible. Stalin had been a Georgian too. Someone else it hadn't been good to be noticed by.

Aurelian peeked around the corner to see the bald bodyguard and one of the smaller ones pick up an older addict in his sixties. Up close they looked distressingly large, especially next to the addict. His emaciated chest rose and fell with effort, and his arms looked like they could easily slip through their beefy fists. Like they were trying to hold a noodle. Coba took a metal case from his overcoat, about the size of a paperback book. It had stenciled red markings on it that looked like Soviet military. From the case he pulled out a hypodermic needle. Coba paused to look at it with great respect, and then moved a half-step forward towards the junkie. Aurelian turned away just as Coba sank the needle into the addict's arm and pushed the plunger.

That didn't make any sense. What drug dealer would give a free drug to someone already addicted?

"Stop wriggling, you old bastard," came one of the younger men's voices. Then Aurelian heard a sudden scream, followed by a rattling moan. That was all the confirmation he needed to decide it was far past time to leave. He put on his backpack and prepared to run.

"Tell me where the basket is," Coba demanded.

Basket? Aurelian wondered. Was that some kind of code word or something?

"We... we don't know..." said a scratchy voice. It must have been coming from the skinny old addict. It was unexpectedly coherent, and also strange, as if more than one person was speaking at once.

"Find where," said Coba, "and I will let you have this one."

The apparently crazy old junkie proceeded to argue with himself. The argument ceased, and then every single hair on Aurelian's neck leapt to attention. It felt as if someone stood right next to him, and was staring. He whirled around to check behind him, and saw only junkies gazing into space.

"He knows something about the basket," the addict outside said.

"Who?" said Coba impatiently. "You're pointing the body's arm at the upstairs wall."

"The young man just around the corner on the landing. Aurelian Vyzhivshiy."

Aurelian felt his own jaw drop. How could anyone here know his real name? Pavel didn't even know it!

The heavy footsteps of a bodyguard plodded up the stairs. With no other options, Aurelian stayed crouched and waited until the footsteps were just around the corner. Then he leaped blindly at where the man should be, and rammed his elbows into the chest of a man the size of a bear. Somehow his luck held for once. It had been the medium-sized bodyguard, and he was knocked off balance. The man stumbled, and Aurelian slammed a foot into his side and knocked him back a step. As he fumbled at the top of the stairs and lost his footing, Aurelian rushed past him down the stairs.

The two other bodyguards still had their hands somewhat full with the addict they'd picked up off the stairs. The largest one of the three acted quickly enough to let go of the old junkie and throw a ham-sized fist at Aurelian's head, the wind whistling as it barely missed. It raised Aurelian's adrenalin even more, and helped him to barely manage not being there for its intended follow up, and instead sink a punch right into the guard's crotch.

By this time the third bodyguard had let go of the old man and pulled out a gun, letting the addict fall like a sack of paste.

Aurelian jumped over the side of the banister. Used to second story exits, he rolled with the impact and shot to his feet, already heading for the front door. "Wait!" Aurelian heard Coba bellow from the stairs. Whatever the coroner-turned-pusher was about to say, Aurelian didn't even waste time to wonder. He hit the cold air of dusk and kept running.

The area was poor and suburban, and offered little cover. Another house or yard wouldn't work. It was time to zigzag through the roads and woods and disappear.

But to where?

If only the damned museum job hadn't gone so bad. He had a place to stay above the store of his mentor in thieving, Volya. It was not much, just a cot in a locked room. Now he couldn't even trust his own bed from police surveillance. It also was just not right to risk police attention on the old man. Volya hadn't exactly saved him out of kindness, but a debt was still a debt.

The place didn't have much besides the cot, just some clothes and some books Aurelian had planned someday to read. He could get more books someday. What he missed right now was its warmth.

An hour and a half and nearly two miles later, Aurelian had made it to a more populated area with various soviet-area housing projects. He saw no immediate police, pursuers or robbers, so he felt it safe to slow his pace and start to seek a hole to hide in.

Curse this city. He'd been stuck in St. Petersburg for ten years. Russia was supposed to no longer be a dictatorship, yet still there was no way to even leave one city without an official passport to another. He could not even apply, or they would find out he didn't have a passport for St. Petersburg.

All he wanted was a way to get to Moscow. There were gangsters there too, like everywhere. Especially in the government. Still, there he could make real money. Maybe even go legitimate and find work that wasn't hurting others or himself. Here, too much risk for far too little reward. Moscow, that was the dream. Moscow was the gold medal, St. Petersburg was the silver, and there was no bronze.

Frostbite and exposure could kill him just as dead as any bullet. He needed some place to stay warm enough to live until dawn. If this were an American movie about Russia, he might come across some strangers congregating around a fire in a barrel. It must not be that cold in America. No one stayed out at night in alleys here, let alone with barrels to indulge in luxurious public fires. His best bet was to find an apartment building and work from there.

He began to search the block of apartment buildings. Eventually he found one that looked occupied and not too posh, with a trash alley up the side blocked by a fence. It would not do to go in the front entrance. He checked and saw no one observing him, then hopped the fence and ran along the building's side until he reached a fire exit. A quick picked lock and he found himself inside a dark stairwell. He closed his eyes completely for a few seconds so they would adjust, and opened them.

There appeared to be no basement, so he went the opposite direction and headed for the roof. Near the top was a side door that yielded easily to Aurelian's skills. Inside there was a fairly large and empty space. The floor was dirty, but it was at least dry. At the far end was apparently a maintenance man's refuge - a crate, a couple of pornographic magazines and what looked like an electric space heater.

That should give off enough heat that he would not die of the cold. He should be happy his luck held this far at all. He plugged in the heater, set down his backpack and leaned against the wall to drink in the heater's comforting warmth. In just a few more hours he could at least be free of this city.

He had just leaned his head back to try and catch some rest, when he was shocked upright by a crawling sensation all over his neck and head. It was the same feeling as he'd had in the drug house. He looked around frantically. There was no one and nothing near him that he could see.

"There," he heard a voice outside, just past the room's door. A moment later it was kicked open.

It was Coba and his three bears. The bodyguards drew guns, and fixed them on Aurelian. The largest one, the one he'd kicked at the top of the stairs, came towards him. He looked rather angry, probably at how easily Aurelian had slipped past him.

Aurelian had no option but to look as calm as he could. "Help you?" he asked, rising to his feet as nonchalantly as he could.

Coba looked at him for a second, and then laughed. "So cool, so cool," he added. "Mr. Vyzhivshiy, let's talk about some things."

"And spread your arms in the air while you do it," growled the biggest bodyguard. "You won't be able to sneak a punch this time."

Aurelian felt his defiance rise, even as he raised his hands. "What, I should give you warning? Have you seen how big you are?"

"I'm not here to discuss boxing rules," said Coba. "Where is the basket?"

Aurelian shook his head. "No bullshit. I really don't know what you're talking about."

Coba sighed, and pointed to the bodyguard Aurelian had kicked at the top of the stairs. "Vasily, check his backpack."

Aurelian examined the man as he holstered his gun and walked over. He was clearly professional, taking care not to cross the first bear's line of sight. Pragmatic, Aurelian gave the man no resistance as he took off Aurelian's backpack and dumped its contents onto the room's filthy floor.

The man poked through all Aurelian had in the world. It didn't take long. "Not here," he said.

"Disappointing," said Coba. "Where is it?"

"I don't even know what you're looking for, how can I know where it is?"

Coba shook his head impatiently. "Don't waste my time. I have it on very good authority you are connected to the basket."

Aurelian laughed as if the matter were light as falling snow. "What authority? Because they apparently know something I don't know."

"That authority with no reason to lie," growled the larger, angrier bodyguard. "The dead, who you will soon join."

"Nikolai, be quiet," said Coba. "Aurelian, just tell us where the basket is, and I will let you leave my city on the *Visigoth* at dawn."

Aurelian tried to keep his face from showing the shock he felt. How had this man known his plans to that degree—down to the name of the ship? He attempted to master his growing dismay. "If there is some connection I have to some basket, I am not aware of it. If you know my plans to that degree, you should know that too."

Coba considered him. "It is strange that there aren't more details for that," he admitted. "Still my...sources have never lied." He nodded to his men. "Bring him. We will sort this out." The ex-coroner turned his back and ventured to leave.

Aurelian looked at the approaching bodyguards as calmly as he could. His odds were bad enough in this enclosed room. Once they took him God knows where, his odds of survival shrank to microscopic levels.

The giant Nikolai pointed his gun at Aurelian's legs, and smiled. "Try to run," he sneered. "I would quite enjoy that." The bodyguard named Vasily approached behind him, took Aurelian's left arm down from its raised position, and then took his right forearm to cuff it.

Aurelian dropped and then spun to his right, grabbing and turning the second bodyguard with him. Nikolai fired, but didn't hit Aurelian. Instead a wet splash of blood erupted from the side of Vasily's kneecap. He screamed in pain as Aurelian threw him at the first bear and ran for the door.

Aurelian's luck almost held. But as he dodged past the third bodyguard, the man shoved his side with just enough impact to push Aurelian into the room's wall. This gave Nikolai enough time to catch him by the back of his head and then pull his arm behind his back.

The bastard increased pressure on Aurelian's arm until it almost broke. Aurelian gasped.

"You like that, bug?" the giant asked, smiling as if he was picking flowers.

"Fuck your mother!" Aurelian said through gritted teeth.

"Your grandmother Irina says hello," said Nikolai, and laughed.

Aurelian stared. He hadn't spoken of his grandmother to anyone in almost ten years! How did this stranger know her name?

"Good night, cockroach." Their conversation concluded, he introduced Aurelian's head to the wall and then to darkness.

AURELIAN AWOKE TO find himself looking at a broken vial held in a soft and slender hand. The vial was the sort that was used to wake people up. The hand looked female. The world was also on its side.

He realized he was lying on a bed. His eyes trailed from the hand up its arm to the hand's owner, a slim young woman with a graceful form. Her long black hair fell on either side of a simple white dress. Her deep brown eyes looked back at him.

As his consciousness returned she moved back, sat in a nearby chair and looked away, examining her nails. "You're a mess," she said.

He moved his head first, and then his arms. His hands weren't tied. He looked down at his own jacket. Apparently some of the floor's filth had gotten on it, as well as some dried blood. He touched the side of his head, and winced. He felt it again, more carefully. A rather nasty scrape, but nothing seemed broken.

"Yes, he is a mess," agreed the voice to his left. Aurelian was disappointed but not surprised. There was the bodyguard who'd knocked him out, as sure as life's injustice. "Go tell Mikhail he is awake," the bear ordered.

"I woke him up. You go tell him," she responded, and began filing her nails.

Nikolai growled. "Do you want to find out who is in charge here?"

She returned his gaze with cold indifference. "I believe I

already know. Would you like to find out which of us is more expendable?"

Aurelian saw a vein start to pulse in the man's forehead, but heard only silence. After a moment Nikolai stood up and left the room.

"What do you do here?" Aurelian asked.

"What I don't do is answer your questions," she said.

Mikhail Coba entered the room. Nikolai followed, pushing a decrepit man who moved with awkward, shuffling steps. This walking husk looked even worse than the last addict Aurelian had seen them interrogating.

He realized it was someone he knew. "Pavel?" Aurelian asked softly.

Coba chuckled. "You knew him? Well there's not much of him left. But we'll get as much as we can before we start a new one."

Pavel's skin was turning colors as they spoke, spots of deep unhealthy red spreading and slowly changing at the edges to greens and purples. From his mouth came short puffs of breath, each seeming another gasp of life fleeing his body.

"Those inside, come to the surface," Coba commanded.

"Aurelian," the voice came from the addict's mouth. "You must tell them." Pavel's voice sounded more than a little odd. Yet some part of the oddness was so familiar. Aurelian didn't like it at all.

"Pavel, stop playing around to get your fix. These guys are serious," He faced Mikhail. "What garbage is this? This junkie knows nothing about me."

"The junkie isn't talking," Coba said. "Listen harder."

"Aurelian," the voice continued to emerge from Pavel's sinking face. "Remember our summers in the country? Before I had to die." The voice broke. "Do as this Coba says.

Let me leave this world to find peace. Don't make me see you die too."

Aurelian's jaw dropped.

It was his grandmother's voice. He had attended her funeral ten years ago, before he ran away from his so-called home, never to return.

"Tell us, idiot!" Nikolai bellowed. Aurelian turned towards the sound of the bodyguard's voice out of instinct, but the words didn't really register. He slowly turned back to Pavel's dying form.

"Tell him!" continued the voice of his long-dead grandmother, continuing to mix oddly with Pavel's voice. "Tell him where the basket is, so I can be free!"

Aurelian shook his head. "What kind of shit is—?"

"Yes, this is really happening," Coba cut in, with a bored tone of having said things many times before. "Where is the basket?"

Aurelian swallowed. "What basket?"

Coba slapped him. "You don't appear to be concussed. Try harder."

Aurelian stared. He tried to speak, and words failed him. He tried again. "You bring me here—after teaching that, that crawling, crippled snake to reproduce the voice of my dead grandmother? And you ask me about a basket?"

"He is not too quick, this one," the girl said.

Defiance rose in Aurelian's mind, giving him an anchor to cling to in this storm of unreality. "Fuck you, bitch, no one asked you shit. Maybe you should hear a cheap imitation of your dead grandmother and have stupid questions thrown at you, then you can talk."

"I hear everyone's dead grandmother," she said, and went back to filing her nails.

"Good for you," said Aurelian. He faced Coba. "I don't

have any reason to lie to you, and I don't have any idea what you're talking about. However you're doing these stupid parlor tricks, they're a waste of time. I'm a thief, and a good one. I don't steal baskets."

Coba examined him thoughtfully. "You inside the husk, he seems to be telling the truth. Explain this."

Another voice spoke from Pavel's voice box. "He knows something he does not know. He is connected. Perhaps someone else he knows, knows more. We have done all we can. Let us feed!"

"Stop playing games, Pavel, or I'll break your fucking neck!" Aurelian yelled.

Coba caught Nikolai's eye, and indicated Aurelian. "Go to my police contacts, and find his known associates."

Nikolai looked a bit relieved. "I shall go check right now."

Mikhail held up a finger. "Not just yet. See this before you go. It's a little different every time." He smiled at Aurelian. "You watch also, thief. It is most instructive." He addressed what Aurelian had once known as Pavel. "Our bargain is complete. You may feed."

A deep sigh emerged from Pavel's face, that Aurelian could swear had the tone of many voices. Pavel's body then began to crumble from within. A smoke emerged from his form as the bones beneath his skin fell in on themselves. His body didn't drop so much as it gradually lost the mass to stand. The smell was the most disturbing of all—a dry, ashy smell, with no life left in it. The last to go was his skin, some of which remained in a pile mixed in with the man's clothes.

Aurelian looked at the remains, and then to the bodyguard. Their eyes met, for once without anger or contempt. Nikolai's face held a deep revulsion that could only come from seeing such a thing many times before.

Coba smiled with satisfaction. "Just so you know what kind of man I am, and what I can do."

"What those spirits you deal with can do," the girl corrected.

Coba glared at her for a moment, then resumed as if she hadn't spoken. "Thief, you had better search that scrambled young mind of yours and tell me how to find this. It is a wicker basket, brown, and about sixty years old. It will have a bit of red paint on the inside near the handle, which covers a hidden pocket."

The girl spoke. "You will have a better chance of surviving if you accept that this is real. Not a great chance, but at least better."

Aurelian put a great amount of effort into it, and managed to clear his mind. "I need to speak again with that —that thing that says it is my grandmother," he said finally.

"You should not ask for that," said the girl.

Coba smiled. "We can arrange that. But not just yet. Lyita, it is time for you to earn some of your keep."

Lyita stood, and put her fingernail file on the chair behind her. "I hate you," she said, in the same flat tone as a butcher might say "That slice of meat will cost you seven rubles."

"What is this even about?" asked an agitated Aurelian. "You can at least tell me that! How will that harm you?"

"Very well," Coba's eyes sparkled. "One day, when I was still a coroner, a body came across my table - so old and melted, it seemed it must have laid there for centuries. Yet from a journal in his coat pocket, he had died just a day before. In his notes I read rumors and hints of a project long ago. With the help of my criminal associates, I broke into his apartment and found the drug which killed him. Used sparingly, it enables me to do this." He waved at Pavel's remains. "Summon ghosts to worthless flesh like his. Where, in return for the joy of human sensation, they quickly take over a body and make it follow my commands." he rubbed his hands. "If a man like cannot be useful while living, he will be made useful before he is consumed. This fate awaits you, if you keep me from what I want."

The older man reached inside his coat.

Aurelian launched off the cot to grab what Coba reached for, and barely caught it by his fingertips. It was the same case he'd seen back at Coba's drug house. Coba dived to grab it back but missed. Aurelian scrambled to open it, and retrieved the only syringe inside. Just in time he held it needle first at Coba, who backed away.

Fear bloomed in the old man's eyes. "Be careful. You don't know what you're doing with that."

"Just stay back!" warned Aurelian. "Or you'll see how much you like it!"

"Get out of my way, sir!" Nikolai declared as he drew his gun.

"That's the last one, don't let him waste it!" Coba demanded.

Aurelian held the needle against the wall. "I'll smash it, how's that? You'd better let me out of here."

The bodyguard placed a large hand on Coba's shoulder and easily moved him to one side, using his other hand to point his gun at Aurelian's face. He held it still and advanced slowly. "How are you going to get out of here and keep that needle against the wall, cockroach?"

"I'll trade you the gun for it."

The bodyguard gave vent to a short bark of laughter. "I'm not an idiot."

Aurelian didn't argue the point. "Drop your ammo clip,

and give me the gun. I'll give you the needle and leave. I don't need to be a part of any of this crap."

"Just get the needle back, dammit!" Coba screamed.

Nikolai paused, and came to a decision. He held his left hand out to Aurelian palm forward, and with his right had pointed his gun to the ceiling. He pressed the clip release on the gun, grabbed the clip and pocketed it. Then he flipped the gun, and offered it grip-first to Aurelian.

Aurelian very carefully reached forward for the gun, with his other hand still holding the needle against the wall.

The bodyguard dropped the gun, grabbed Aurelian's wrist, and yanked him forward.

Guessing what was coming next, Aurelian got the needle in front of his face just before the giant's fist came in. The needle stabbed deep into the flesh between Nikolai's knuckles and the plunger was pushed in from the force.

"No!" said the man, jumping back with sudden shock and staring at the syringe now protruding from his hand. "No!"

"Damn you!" said Coba.

The bodyguard fell to the ground and began to twitch. Just as with the old junkie in the drug house, he gave vent to a bloodcurdling scream.

Aurelian grabbed the gun, snatched the ammo clip from the twitching man's pocket, and slammed it back into the handle. He aimed at Coba. "Get out of the way. I'm leaving."

"You wasted it!" cried Coba. "You'll pay for this!"

"Keep talking. I have the gun." Aurelian turned to the girl. "Let's go!"

She blinked. "What for? He will just find you again. Your grandmother's ghost will know."

"How did you get involved in this?" Aurelian demanded.

"He has my parents' souls under his thumb. Same as your grandmother."

Aurelian stared at Coba and went pale. "Is that what you are doing, you damn vulture? The one good woman in my life?"

Coba sneered. "Yes. Kill me and she doesn't even go to Hell. She stays unliving and alone in St. Petersburg for all eternity."

Aurelian's finger tightened on the trigger.

He just couldn't bring himself to do it. Coba smiled.

"Just stay away from me!" Aurelian yelled, and fled upstairs.

It was the same drug dacha. Here was the same living room he'd run through last night. The other two bodyguards were lounging on couches, engaged with a couple of low-grade whores. The kind who didn't mind the ambiance of people dying in their own filth as long as they weren't competition for the coke. The slightly larger of the two, the bodyguard named Vasily, now had a heavy bandage on his leg. He saw Aurelian and reached for his gun, to be stopped by a warning motion from Aurelian.

"I'd check on your boss if I were you!" he yelled at them. That seemed to stall them just long enough for him to make the corner of the hallway and hit the door.

Out he ran, this time into morning sunlight. There were a couple of civilians on the street, probably on their way to jobs that might even be honest. He hid the gun inside his jacket and walked quickly, looking for a crowd he might be able to fade into. He found small but sufficient amount of people waiting at a bus stop. A bus pulled up and he entered by the back door, hoping that he would not be asked to pay.

The bus was headed to the center of the city. He found a seat and gathered his thoughts as best he could. Once again he was out in the open, this time without even any of his possessions. His last way out of the city was gone — the ship must have sailed hours ago. His old cot above Volya's place was as bad a thought as ever.

There was only one thing he could try. Find the first payphone he could, and call the Finnlander. He realized he couldn't even afford that. He lacked even the coin to pay for this bus ride. Could his luck let up on him once? What kind of gypsy had he screwed over to deserve this? That brought him uncomfortably close to thinking about his dead grand-mother. He stuffed those thoughts deep inside. They were useless right now.

He needed to contact the Finnlander. How?

He placed his hand over the gun's cold metal in his coat pocket. It gave him a feeling of security. It was also the only thing he had that was worth any money at all. He was going to have to either rob someone with it or sell it. By personal preference and by skills, he was a thief but not a robber.

He got off just outside the city center, and began search-ing. It was harder to find fellow criminals in the morning, but after some time he managed to locate a man interested in his stolen .45. The money was an insulting pittance, but he now could make a call.

He found one of the few remaining payphone booths in a dumpy bar that was just opening for an incoming crowd of laborers, and called the Finnlander. The man picked up on the third ring.

"Hello," said Aurelian. "Is Alexandra there?" This was their prearranged code if they got separated after the robbery, which they had been—by police that came way too quickly, thanks to the Finnlander's failure to retrieve the right alarm codes.

"She's at the opera. Can I help you with something?"

"There's a book I need. Can you bring it to the corner of Gubina and Promyshlennya?" By previous agreement, any places mentioned on the phone were off by five blocks north and three blocks west.

"Sure," said the Finnlander, in a baffled sort of tone. "What book?"

"Any book," Aurelian snapped. "Just bring it." Then he realized something. "Do you happen to have any baskets?"

"No," the surprised voice said. "Just—well this old wicker thing that came with the apartment. You've seen it before."

"Bullshit!" said Aurelian.

"On the mantelpiece. You knocked it over when you were drunk, and complained about how old and dirty it was. Why?"

Aurelian did remember it—a worthless-looking wicker piece of shit, dry and cracking with age.

"Burn that basket," he said. "I'm not joking. Do it right now."

"Why?"

"You wouldn't believe me if I told you. Just do it! And stay away from Coba!"

"Coba? Are you involved with him?"

Aurelian closed his eyes. "I don't want to be."

"That's good, don't contact him," said the Finn. "I hear he has many contacts in the police. Also it's whispered he killed his wife and daughter to make his life more simple. You're better off if he never even learns your name."

"I'll keep that in mind," Aurelian said numbly. "Just meet me in half an hour."

He hung up and left the bar. By hurrying, he was able to reach a corner near the meeting spot in fifteen minutes. He bided his time in constant movement, sneaking looks at the meeting site once a minute.

Seven minutes before they were supposed to meet, he saw the Finnlander arrive. The man was doing the same thing that Aurelian had been, checking around early to see if anyone else might be seeing them. The Finn also held a brown paper bag.

Aurelian was about to wave and catch his eye—when he saw the Finn look behind and give a light nod. Aurelian followed his glance, and saw a parked black van. Of the shadowy shapes showing through the windshield, one looked just like...

Aurelian's fists clenched. The bastard had sold him out to Coba. From the mere mention of Coba's name! Had Finn just sold them all out at the museum robbery too? Was that why the alarms had gone off, and why the Finn himself hadn't gone into hiding?

Then Aurelian felt that cold feeling all along the back of his neck again. He ran through the city's streets, not knowing where he should even go.

After another fifteen minutes of running his side began to ache. He found a place behind a parked delivery truck. He hoped at least to have a few minutes here before he would need to run again.

Where previously he had been in the position of choosing between jail or a ship that could take him to Odessa...he was now in the position of choosing between jail and death.

They could apparently find him no matter what. If he was in jail, at least Coba might not be able to get to him. Perhaps Aurelian would only get a couple of years, and not be put in with too many murderers. Maybe, just maybe, if his luck held to a degree it never had before, whatever this strangeness was would all blow over by the time his sentence was done.

There was nothing else to it. Any other decision was just increasing the chance Coba would catch him first.

He sighed and walked towards the nearest police station. He knew where it was by heart, after having avoided it as much as he could since he'd first come to this city. It took less time to get there than he'd expected. Or maybe he was just enjoying his last breaths of free air too much.

On the last corner before the station stood Lyita, waiting for him. He knew what else must be waiting, and looked around until he found it. At the opposite corner was a black van, with Vasily leaning against it on his good leg as he smoked. Inside the van there would no doubt be Coba himself, and perhaps the Finnlander was well.

They were still in public and in daylight. Even with Coba's police connections, Aurelian doubted they would try to kidnap or shoot him here. In any case his best odds still applied. Jail over death.

He walked forward, and Lyita moved in front of him. "Out of my way."

"I cannot," Lyita said. "He has my parents' souls."

"Not my problem."

"He has your grandmother too."

"Bullshit!" Aurelian snarled. "Out of my way!"

"You now will see why Coba keeps me." She stiffened, and her eyes rolled back in her head to show pure white. Her posture softened to that of an old woman stooped with the weight of hard years.

"Aurelian," he heard his grandmother's voice again. This time it was mixed with Lyita's voice, and with less harshness. "You must not go to jail. You will die!"

"I will fucking kill you, Lyita!" Aurelian shouted. A

couple of passersby looked their way. "I don't care anymore. I'm going to jail anyway!"

"Everyone must die, Grandson. But you mustn't so soon, and not for this. This girl will die too, and many others after her, all for nothing - to then be trapped like me."

Deep in his bones he knew it was her. No one could have possibly known her mannerisms, her tones, the look in her eyes. So many things he had not even remembered until now, shown on this younger woman's frame like a movie on a screen. "How can this be?"

"I don't know the how. It is."

"What has been done to you?"

"I am stuck between worlds," his grandmother's voice was laden with despair. "After my death I could feel the beyond freedom, whether it was something or nothingness. Before I could reach out to it, I was drawn into a prison instead. I touch nothing, taste nothing, feel nothing, see and hear nothing. I can only break free for moments, to inhabit someone else's flesh, like I am now." Lyita's solid white eyes began to wet. "You cannot imagine what this is like. You cannot let him keep doing this to me. You cannot let him do this to others. We dead cannot rest until we're free." Tears that were not Lyita's rolled down her cheeks. "I named you, you know."

He laughed in spite of himself, tears starting in his own eyes. He remembered that story now. "You said 'Aurelian' was from church Latin. I was your little golden one."

She pointed a finger at him. "Aurelian was a Roman emperor, towards the end of their empire. He tried as best he could. You were a good boy once. Do the right thing. Do not die giving up. You will only join us in our torture as one ashamed." Her voice softened. "I would not have that for you, Grandson. I will not allow it."

Aurelian said nothing as Lyita's posture returned to that of a young woman, now a bit shaken. Her eyes returned to normal, and she wiped away the tears that were not hers.

They stood staring at each other for a second.

Wearily, Aurelian walked to the waiting van.

Vasily the bodyguard sneered, tossed aside his cigarette, wincing as the routine motion put unexpected weight on his newly wounded leg. The cigarette died with a quick puff in the snow as he hobbled around the van and slid the cargo door open. Aurelian stepped in, to find waiting for him on bench seats Coba, the Finnlander as he'd half-expected... and what was once Nikolai.

"He knows we're not who this body was," a voice cackled. The eyes of Nikolai's former body were bloodshot, and the skin around them had begun to take on a greenish tinge. "Hee hee! The fear he has! We love this! It's been so long... please more healthy bodies Coba..."

Vasily slid the door shut, and made his way to the driver's seat. "Straight to the dig," Coba declared. They took off. It was too late for Aurelian to reconsider now.

Coba faced Aurelian. "I didn't expect you would think of going straight to jail. That was almost clever. It still would not have stopped me of course."

Aurelian tried to shrug, hemmed in as he was by hopelessness. "Why do you even need me along?"

"You will find out soon enough."

"Fuck you, you pimp of the dead."

Far from offended, Coba laughed. He turned to the Finnlander. "Do you have it?"

The Finn opened the bag to show the crappy wicker basket Aurelian had seen when he was drunk.

"I told you to get rid of that, you fool!" Aurelian exclaimed.

The Finn gave him a superior smile. "You never did understand business." He handed the tired-looking object to Coba, who produced a pocket knife and began to probe inside it.

Something else clicked into place for Aurelian. "You went back after the bust, and stole art for yourself!"

"Yes, after the police took care of the partners I'd have to split it with." The Finn laughed. "You all thought yourselves so smart."

Aurelian lunged at Coba, to stuff that laugh down his throat. He was pushed back by the Nikolai-thing's big hands.

Coba laughed. "You petty thieves squabble over trinkets, as we near the potential of truly great reward...Ah! " He ripped open the dried and brittle wicker, to reveal a strip of paper. It had a series of numbers in faded black ink. "At last!" Coba looked at it for a moment with pure love, and put it inside his suit. He rubbed his hands. "This will all work so well!"

The van slowed to a stop. The bodyguard named Vasily turned around from the driver's seat, to point a gun straight at him. Coba took this moment to hand Aurelian some handcuffs.

"Put these on. Behind your back." Aurelian hesitated only as long as it took for the bodyguard to nudge the air with his gun. "You too, Lyita. It will make those pretty breasts of yours pop out quite appealingly." She looked at Coba as if he was some entirely new form of filth she'd found stuck to her shoe.

The Finn coughed. "Now, about my payment."

"Indeed." Coba produced another pair of handcuffs and tossed them onto the Finn's lap.

Aurelian had the small but still substantial satisfaction of seeing the Finn's eyes gape wide. "We had a deal!"

Coba shrugged. "An old snake does not keep deals with young snakes. That is how a snake gets to be old."

"Can I just kill him?" asked the altered Nikolai. It giggled in childish glee. "I so would like to kill him!"

"If he doesn't put those cuffs on, do whatever you like." Coba fixed the Finn with a stare. Red-faced, the Finn put on the handcuffs.

Aurelian, Lyita and the Finn were led out of the van in the now late-morning sun. It was warm for a winter's day in St. Petersburg, only ten degrees below freezing. They were in the courtyard of some abandoned apartment building among many at the eastern edge of the city, where few even bothered to squat.

"In there." Coba pointed to a doorway. Aurelian wondered if they were being marched in to die.

They came into the small living room of some Soviet bureaucrat's former apartment. On an abandoned bookcase lay several miner's helmets. In the middle of the room was a large hole cut through the floor and into apparent dirt below, with a cheap ladder poking out. A hint of a smell came up from the hole, a vile perfume that mixed mildew and...the smell Pavel's body had given as he was eaten by the ghosts.

Coba pointed to the bodyguard named Vasily. "Lead the way."

"On this leg?" he protested.

"Do you want to partake in the rewards or not?"

The wounded bodyguard cursed, and hobbled over to the abandoned bookcase. He took one of the miner's helmets, and threw the other to Coba.

"What happened to your third bear?" asked Aurelian, with nothing to lose.

"Shut it," Vasily snarled.

"We'll find him soon enough," said Coba. He pulled a gun from the confines of his coat. "First things first."

"He didn't like what we do with this body," said the thing called Nikolai. It giggled. "Maybe he can be our next feast."

Vasily turned his helmet light on, holstered his gun and started awkwardly down the ladder, favoring his wounded leg.

"Now you." Coba motioned to Aurelian with his own gun.

This was worse than the last time Aurelian had been trapped in a room with them. If he had to die, he would rather it was up here.

Lyita's eyes pleaded with him. His grandmother's most recent words stayed with him.

Silently Aurelian went over to the pit in the middle of the room, and climbed down the ladder. He was followed by Lyita. Behind her was the Finn, the ghoulish remains of Nikolai, and finally Coba.

The ladder descended through a rough dirt tunnel into a chamber. Aurelian jumped the last ten feet and whirled around, hoping to catch Vasily by surprise. The bodyguard was ready for him, and sneered from across the room with his weapon back in hand.

Aurelian sighed and examined the rest of the room. Vasily's helmet lamp illuminated concrete floors and a roughly poured concrete floor. At the far end of the room was a spiral staircase made of rusting steel.

The rest of their strange company came down the ladder. Vasily went first down the stairs, and with without words they followed, deeper into the earth. Aurelian wondered if the stairwell would continue to withstand their weight. He and Lyita were light at least. If Coba, his servants or Finn fell through it wouldn't exactly break his heart.

Unfortunately, while still rusty in some places the staircase was altogether sturdy.

He began to hear giggling from the thing that once was Nikolai. "It's here, we're almost here. This body can get in, we can free our souls!"

"Do be quiet," Coba commanded.

A second voice from the giant body muttered, "Or what?" It was immediately answered by a third voice from the same body, "Shh, not now." A fourth voice agreed, "We're so close."

Aurelian wondered if Coba heard the exchange. If he were Coba this discussion would begin to concern him.

They came to the end of the stairs, and faced a cavernous darkness. Coba flicked on a battery-powered work light, illuminating a room about a hundred feet wide and thirty feet high. The floor was concrete and dusty, the ceiling reinforced with steel girders.

On the wall immediately facing them was a large stencil in red letters. The text read "Special Department 19 - Ghost Magnet". In the center was an upside down red star.

It looked familiar. Aurelian realized he had seen the same insignia on the metal case of needles that Coba had flourished, back in the dacha where this journey had begun.

Coba's and the guards gun and the Nikolai-thing's giggling nudged them forward. They soon reached the other end of the room, and a door that would do credit to a bank vault.

The walls contained some murals, including a rather grim mural showing the Supreme Soviet encircling the world. Aurelian had a clearer notion of this entire space now. This could only be intended to impress any visitors who'd come here with the fruits of whatever secret budget had created this facility.

That meant the purpose of this place was most likely beyond that door. The smell of death was slightly stronger – unless it was just that they were in close quarters with Coba's ghoulish bodyguard.

"What's this?" asked the Finn.

"This is where you die, hee hee," said the bodyguard.

"Shush," said Coba, in bored tones. He pointed to Aurelian and the Finn. "You two fools stand against the vault."

"Like shit!" said Aurelian. Vasily slammed the butt of his pistol into the side of Aurelian's head. Dazed, he fell halfway to the ground. He twisted and jumped back up, ramming his shoulder directly into the man's gut right below his sternum. Vasily flew backward, slamming into the wall himself. His pistol went off, ricocheting the bullet around the room. Everyone ducked as the bullet bounced and chips of concrete went flying.

Aurelian kicked at the man's bandaged kneecap. The man screamed in pain and leveled a gun directly at Aurelian.

"Stop!" said Coba. "Don't kill him yet. Are you crazy? We need them both alive. Unless you want to take his place?"

"Stop with your bullshit," Vasily shot back. "I don't understand every crazy thing that's going on here, but this street trash dies."

The massive bodyguard now owned by ghosts stepped between them. It paused a moment, then reached out with blinding speed and grasped the guard's hand and twisted it upwards.

"It feels so good to move flesh!" one of it's voices said.

"Careful, you'll rip these muscles moving them that fast," came another.

"So use them up!" chimed in a third.

"It feels so good to have flesh again!" declared yet another voice.

Vasily tried to free his hand from the possessed giant's fist, and found he could not. With his free arm he punched the creature in the stomach. A volume of air emerged from its open mouth, and then a small bit of puke.

The giant's only reaction was to smile. "Yes! Make us feel some more! Pain is wonderful. Feeling anything is wonderful."

"Later," ordered Coba. "Give Vasily's gun to me, and let him go."

The giant sighed in several voices at once, and snatched the gun from Vasily. The creature then tossed the gun to Coba, and shoved the bodyguard away. It laughed as Vasily stumbled and fell backwards, to bounce off the wall and hit the floor.

What was once Nikolai's head swung down to examine the hands of the body they possessed, and smiled in satisfaction as it closed them into fists. The creature then smiled at the downed bodyguard.

Coba addressed the downed bodyguard. "Vasily. You! Cripple. Look at me." Vasily dragged his eyes away from the horror's smile with some effort. "Get up and uncuff Aurelian and that Finnlander, if you know what's good for you."

The bodyguard managed to climb to his feet, hobbled over and uncuffed Aurelian and then the Finn.

"Now, each of you fools stand on one of those plates." Coba pointed at the floor near the vault door. Aurelian saw two metal semicircles that extended from beneath the vault's door.

"You stand there," said Aurelian.

Coba sighed and addressed the giant. "Hold them there.

I promise you all the bodies you could ever want. If this succeeds, we will all have our needs fulfilled."

The former bodyguards' former hands grabbed Aurelian and the Finnlander each by the neck, and held them against the wall over the plates. "Like this?" it said, the body's corrupted breath washing across Aurelian's face and roiled his stomach.

"Yes," said Coba. He went over to a steel beam and examined it briefly, then pressed on a particular rivet. He smiled in satisfaction as, in front of Aurelian and the Finnlander two metal panels slid aside. They held a series of switches with numbers painted next to them.

"Some kind of fuse box?" said Aurelian, baffled.

"Of a sort," Coba chuckled unpleasantly as he produced the strip of paper he'd retrieved from the basket. "This system was set up so that only two authorized people could open it. You two fools have one chance to live through this. Set each switch in front of you to the numbers I tell you, and then pull down the final switch at the same time. If the numbers are wrong or you don't push the switch at the same time, you will both be electrocuted."

"What if we don't help you at all?" said Aurelian.

Coba shrugged. "Then we shoot you both, and Vasily and Lyita give it a try."

Vasily growled. "I strongly advise you to do as he says."

"We had a deal!" the Finnlander said.

"Don't live in the past." Silence filled the small space. "All discussions finished?" Coba turned to the strip of paper. "Enter 5, 17, 7! Then wait for my mark."

Aurelian and the Finn followed his orders. Aurelian hated that his life now depended on the Finnlander. "Listen to me Coba, you son of a bitch. My ass is on the line, so I give the mark."

Coba smiled and nodded, indulgently. "Why not."

Aurelian faced the Finn. "You pull that switch down right when I say 'four'. Not after 'four', but exactly at the same time 'four' leaves my lips. Got it?"

Too fearful for wisecracks or betrayal, the Finn nodded.

"One, two, three, *four!*"

A light charge of electricity came through Aurelian's fingers. He leaped back off of the pad.

In a few seconds there came a light rumbling. Lights turned in the ceiling above the doorway flickered on, and the vault door slid back into the opening behind it. After the first few feet, a track was revealed on the floor. After twenty feet it turned to the side, revealing a cavernous tunnel close to 50 feet high and 200 feet across.

The possessed bodyguard contemptuously pushed Aurelian and the Finn forward.

The tunnel was lined from four to ceiling with circuits, emitting a strange haze and a static hum. Mixed with a smell like sulphur and ozone was the musty smell from decades of stillness —and the same stench that had come from the old junkie, from Pavel and now from Nikolai.

The floor ended abruptly, and the path became dirty and rocks. Railroad tracks began and led onward down the tunnel. Perhaps this was a repurposed mine? As they walked forward they began seeing piles of debris scattered on either side of the tracks. Aurelian realized they were bodies. Easily a dozen of them, long desiccated and fallen into decay. They had not been reached by rats or maggots, and seemed to have mostly melted into the crushed rock and gravel.

The tunnel bended to the left. Along the right side of the tunnel stood an extensive amount of old electronic equipment, with lights and humming sounds indicating they were still in a state operation.

A large downward-pointed red star hung from the ceiling, similar to the core of the insignia they'd seen outside. It was surrounded by a strange glowing blue light, that moved around it like slow motion sparks. Under that light, the star itself looked roughly made from sheet metal but painted with pride, its enamel coating still putting forth a dull shine even today. It looked like the sort of thing very proud techs and scientists would make, in perhaps the only place they could show off and wallow in their pride.

Beyond it the tunnel ended, in a circular platform surrounded by banks of metal cabinets. On the platform's center stood a metal and mesh half sphere about thirty feet in height. The sphere itself was covered in criss-crossed wires and junction boxes. The sphere's base was connected to the floor by several large stacks of wires and components, consisting of wires and tubes and the occasional jumping spark.

The region surrounding the sphere was completed by a shimmering blue light. Arcs of something that looked similar to electricity swirled around it.

Behind the mesh and wires of the sphere there seemed to be a fluid that was very much like what Aurelian had seen inside Coba's hypodermics. Wisps shot through it, at least tens of thousands, numbers impossible to count, moving with what seemed to be their own will. Many of the quick-moving flashes would bang repeatedly into the shimmering blue light on the sphere's exterior, to strike sparks which then repelled them back to the center. Behind the sphere, the tunnel ended in a wall composed of sheet-metal housings. Thick pipes ran from these housings to a console connected to Aurelian's left. Also connecting to this console was a series of conduits running from the half sphere along the floor, running past a ring of seats directly in front of several rows of instrumentation.

Every few moments a wisp would break through and get a few feet past the sphere and then stay there, flickering as if striving against an intense pull. They too would be sucked back into the sphere. At the edge of the shell new wisps would also wink into visibility, while they were already being pulled in.

Aurelian turned and noted Lyita's face. Her eyes were on the sphere itself, and were filled with longing.

"Is that...?" he began.

"Yes, that is where her parents, your grandmother, and many others' souls are kept," said Coba. "Is it not magnificent!"

"What the hell is this?" asked the Finn.

Coba laughed. "Did you not see the sign outside? It is the Ghost Magnet. I knew it was real!" He rubbed his hands together and practically skipped over several mummified corpses to see the device more closely. He briefly basked in its light, and then ran to the console. He ran his hands over the surface of an instrument panel like it was his life's love. He sighed happily. "At last I am here!"

Aurelian noticed that the entire time he never got closer than a certain radius from the sphere. That same region that also was clear of bodies.

Lyita spoke, her voice flat. "Stalin had many secret projects. As he grew closer to death, he became particularly fascinated with souls. He knew how to properly motivate his lessers—he set scientists to conquer death or die. They all failed. This one group found something else by accident — a way to attract and harness the power of ghosts."

"Stalin died before he could use it," said Coba, further

relishing the moment. "All his staff who knew of this project were purged. Now all this is mine."

"And here we are," Vasily agreed. "Now we can really get some power."

"You sons of bitches will rot in seven separate hells," Lyita said without emotion.

Coba chuckled. He walked over to Lyita and took her chin in his hand. "Come now! Don't be petty. Respect the beauty of this moment! Many thousands of psychic freaks like you gave their lives for this. Their brains were harvested for the compounds that help ghosts enter their brains. Now we have not only a new source of that serum - we have the sphere that traps them within itself! I will have an army of ghosts to do my will!"

"Our will," said Vasily.

"Good luck with that," said Aurelian.

"I'm glad I helped," said the Finn. "Would you be interested in a partner? I'm very resourceful. I have so many contacts, you wouldn't believe!"

Coba let go of Lyita, and frowned at Aurelian. "And we almost didn't get here at all, after you wasted that syringe on Nikolai," he added reproachfully.

Aurelian laughed incredulously. "Am I supposed to feel bad about trying to survive?"

"It is fine," said Coba, in a tone magnanimous with victory. "It has all worked out for the best."

"Yes it has!" said the Finn, with forced cheer. "With my help that scumbag Aurelian did not defeat you. Let's end him now so he stays down here!"

"My grandmother died in a hospital in St. Petersburg," Aurelian said with dawning comprehension. "Is that how her soul..."

Coba gave an abrupt dismissal with his hand. "Yes. She

can only escape temporarily to another body, if a mind is open to her—and when that connection ends she is drawn straight back to the Ghost Magnet."

Aurelian saw that the corpses littering the floor wore moldering lab coats. Some appeared to have been partially eaten, perhaps by others. "Whatever happened here, it doesn't seem to have worked out well for these people."

Coba chuckled. "Indeed. When Stalin died, direct knowledge of this facility went with him. These scientists starved to death with no one to come and let them out. Their ghosts must still be in that sphere as well. That basket held the only code in." He shook his head. "So much work to at last find someone living who had seen that basket, and to find had a ghost who knew them. If you had made it onto that freighter the other night, we might not be here at all."

Aurelian saw from the corner of this eye that Finn was edging towards the door. He said nothing. Maybe the surprise of the Finn escaping would give him a chance as well.

Coba shrugged. "I guess that hardly seems lucky to you, now does it? My wife and children also did not feel lucky, when I showed them who was master. The silly debutante found out about my interest, and threatened to report me. A gas accident does wonders for disobedient wives and their child parasites." He gazed off in fond recollection. "I received so much sympathy too—I did enjoy that. But not near as much as I will enjoy this." He clasped his hands behind his back, surveying the premises with joy.

Finn chosen this moment to try to make it to the door. Vasily was not surprised, and pointed his gun straight at the Finn's face. Aurelian's former partner froze, and made a curse.

"We are impatient. What of your promise?" said the voices coming from Nikolai's dying body.

"You will have all the new bodies you desire," said Coba. He looked at Lyita. "You could do nicely." Coba grabbed her.

Aurelian jumped forward. He was stopped by the sight of Coba's pointed gun.

"What of these two thieves?" asked the thing.

"We're done with them," the coroner said. "Enjoy yourself."

The bodyguard grinned from ear to ear. He faced Aurelian, with Finn standing to his right. His right arm moved so quickly it was a blur—punching the Finn so hard in the throat it sounded like his neck snapped. The Finn sank to the floor dead.

It/they looked at Aurelian and smiled wider.

Aurelian stepped back.

"Yes, do run," said a voice from within the bodyguard's frame as it advanced toward Aurelian. "I want to chase him. It's been so long since I felt a body run!"

"I want to feel what it's like kill him with my bare hands!" said another voice. "I never got to do that while I was alive!"

"I did. It wasn't as fun as I thought," said a third voice.

"Shut up! No one asked you," said the first.

"Grandmother, are you in there?" Aurelian asked as he kept moving backward.

"She's not in right now," the first voice said as it followed. It took a deliberate, leisurely pace, as if savoring every moment.

Aurelian had an idea. "Wait! You want to experience sensation again, right? What if you just pleasured yourself?"

The bodyguard's form stopped advancing as they considered this. "You mean...physically?" said one voice.

"Yes, exactly. It must have been a long time since you felt that pleasure," Aurelian said, his voice hopeful.

"He has a point," said another voice.

"We could just rape him," said a third

"True," said the first voice.

"Either during or after we've murdered him?" said a new voice that sounded suspiciously like...

"Pavel?" Aurelian asked. "You son of a bitch!"

"Yes, fine idea," concluded the first voice. The voices having reached agreement, they moved Nikolai's body forward towards Aurelian.

Aurelian searching around for something, anything he could use. Coba sat one of the console's seats, forcing Lyita down next to him. Vasily leaned against an instrument panel and lit a cigarette with an interested expression. He leaned towards Coba and said something too low to hear. Coba laughed and nodded agreement. Lyita's eyes were developing a blank and inward look, before she let her head drop to hide her face in her hair.

Aurelian found a loose section of pipe rusted to the floor, near the outstretched hand of a mummified corpse. He scrambled to pull it loose. The giant nearly caught him just as he pried it free. Aurelian began to swing it. The giant chuckled and tried to grab for it with his arms. Aurelian connected solidly with his forearm. "Yes! The sensation! My arm hurts!" it said joyously.

Hopeless but with not much else to try, Aurelian swung again at the same arm. This time it smacked into the forearm at the elbow. A bone cracked loose, pushing out the cheap suit sleeve at an odd angle. The bodyguard then ran at Aurelian, who barely managed to sidestep it. Nikolai's husk stumbled forward to the wall and put its broken arm in front of it, breaking it further. Enjoying the pain but not distracted by it, the thing spun and charged at Aurelian again.

Aurelian ran and dodged around the room, as it lunged at him with a now useless forearm. Aurelian realized the pipe had a sharp end. Maybe he could stab the thing?

Aurelian noticed a sudden motion across the room. Lyita's head snapped back, her eyes now white orbs. She looked at him and he knew that his grandmother was in there.

"Hit the switch!" she cried.

"What switch?" Aurelian demanded. As his head was turned, the giant connected with a fist across his temple. The force knocked him sideways and left him dazed, causing him to drop the pipe. The creature laughed as it grappled Aurelian and dragged him to the floor.

"With our bare hands now, yes?" the first voice asked.

"Oh yes!" the second voice agreed. The thing's rotting breath washed across his face as it grinned from ear to ear, wrapped its good hand around Aurelian's neck and closing like a vice. Aurelian gasped and struggled, kicking help-lessly. His hands couldn't budge the thing's grip by so much as millimeter.

Aurelian's flailing hand found the pipe again and brought it across the creature's head. It laughed. "Yes! Feeling that! Yes!"

Aurelian swung again, and the thing gave vent to another yelp of joy. His vision started to fade at the edges. He got one knee up under the giant's body, but could not budge its grip. He swung the pipe into the thing's good arm, and felt the pressure loosen. He was dismayed to realize this wasn't due to the impact of the pipe. The thing had been distracted by trying to use the fingers at the end of its broken left arm to loosen its belt and fly.

Swinging again in sheer desperation, Aurelian connected solidly with the thing's good arm at the elbow. The grip on his throat was shaken loose. Gasping for air, Aurelian turned the pipe around and jammed it into the thing's eye. The jagged end slammed through the lower orbital socket, crushing the eye and spreading blood and viscous fluid across the former bodyguard's face.

It jumped back. "I never felt that sensation when I lived!" said a voice excitedly.

"But now we have less vision!" said another. "The bastard has robbed us of half a sense!"

Panicking, Aurelian reversed the pipe and ran the sharp end into the formerly human stomach.

Blood began to pour out and down its front. It frowned. "That has harmed this body."

"Yes! All that pain, it is delicious!"

"We can still kill him before this dies."

It leaned in. Aurelian struggled desperately to pull the pipe loose, but it was firmly lodged inside the former bodyguard's torso.

"Don't kill him just yet!" Pavel's voice came from the former Nikolai's throat. "We can go into his body, if we drag him near the sphere!"

"The switch, Aurelian, the switch!" the voice from Lyita cried. Dazed, Aurelian turned his head to see a large switch to the side of the sphere, several feet past his reach. It was of the type that looked like a gear shift on a car.

The giant lifted him off the ground, perhaps to throw him. Aurelian pulled the pipe free. He could either swing at the creature again, or...

With a prayer from his earliest church-school days on his lips, Aurelian twisted and threw the pipe. It connected with the switch, and knocking it backwards. The humming of wires increased, and the sphere's glow grew stronger. Instead of turning it off, Aurelian had increased the power.

The giant lunged for him as the glowing sphere of energy expanded.

The sphere surround the bodyguard's frame, and the creature lurched and froze. It twisted as voices gripped the throat in protest. One by one short wisps were sucked from the body back into the sphere. The body they had inhabited fell to the ground, still.

Aurelian didn't trust Nikolia when he was human, let alone possessed.

Careful not to enter the glow's radius, Aurelian grabbed the body by the ankle and dragged it towards him. When it was free enough for him to strike, he grabbed the pipe to finish it.

He was stopped midswing by its eyes, returning to humanity once more.

"Thank you..." said Nikolai, as one living human being to another, before he died.

Aurelian watched as a wisp emerged from the body, and was pulled into the glowing sphere to join the other wisps.

Coba gave a sardonic clap. "Ah, you are a resourceful rat. You've cost me a little bit of money." He took a money clip from his pocket, and gave Vasily what looked like 20 rubles. Then Coba drew his gun. "I don't like losing bets. And I definitely don't like rats in my home." He took aim.

"The other way!" his grandmother's voice came from Lyita again. "What you should have done the first time! Set us free!"

"Don't you dare!" yelled Coba. "We don't know what that does!"

Aurelian dove through the glowing haze to the switch,

and pulled it all the way towards him. As he did, something slammed into his back.

The sphere shuddered for a moment, and then stopped all motion.

Then it released. The force exploded across the room, knocking all the living into unconsciousness.

Aurelian awoke first. He saw a somehow familiar floating light flash about him, love and gratitude emanating from it.

He tried to get up, and found his left arm wasn't working right. In the next instant a searing pain revealed itself in his upper back. That bastard Coba must have shot him there.

The blue energetic shell around faded in size intensity. More and more wisps were breaking free.

Moving solely from fear and will, he picked up the pipe in his good arm and wrecked every breakable part of the machinery he could. Then he stabbed through the wire mesh, and heard glass break. Above him and around him, the yellow fluid began draining from the sphere into gratings in the floor.

Aurelian hurried over to where Coba, the two bodyguards, and Lyita lay.

She was alive. Unfortunately, Coba and Vasily were both still breathing too. Not much justice in this world, but he would take what he could get.

He might not have much time to get it. He'd seen first-hand how gunshots affect people. It was a serious thing. He might not have much time left before he went into shock.

He retrieved the handcuff keys from Coba's pocket and uncuffed Lyita. Then he slapped her. "Wake up!" He picked up Coba's gun with his good hand.

A group of wisps that had once been inside the sphere shot into the coroner's body. Coba's eyes opened. "There are enough of us!" said a voice that was not his. "We have him without the serum!"

"Yes!" said another. "Him and his servant. We can make them last. We shall taste our vengeance before we go to freedom!"

"No wait," said a voice that was actually Coba's. "You can't! I'll - I'll give you other people!"

At this moment Vasily's eyes sprang open. "Get out of me!" he screamed.

Lyita came to, and had her own brown eyes again. "What..." She had a couple of wisps around her head as well. Some other flashes of light came near, before her own wisps knocked them away. From the corner of Aurelian's eye, he saw a similar light doing this for him.

"We have to go Lyita," said Aurelian. "Now."

"No!" said Coba's own voice, as the flesh of his face began to wilt. "Don't let them do this. You have to - turn it back on! Suck them back into the machine."

"Or kill us!" said Vasily. "Just don't let us die like this!"

Another voice resumed from Coba's throat. "I think with you two, perhaps we will take our time."

More of the floating lights encircled Coba, and fell into his flesh to disappear. He had no apparent ghosts to fend the others off.

"Maybe your wife and children are already inside you, taking some vengeance," Aurelian said. "Maybe there is some justice."

Aurelian helped Lyita to her feet, nearly falling himself. They walked back through the tunnel towards the chamber's door. His vision almost went black for a moment, and she steadied him.

They made it into the hall outside, and she saw the pairs of fallen handcuffs next to the dead Finn. "One moment!" she said. She ran back inside with them before he could stop her. He lifted the gun and aimed back into the chamber, hoped he wouldn't hit her if he fired. She handcuffed Coba and Vasily together.

She ran back. "Now let's shut the door."

Aurelian agreed, and lent his body to moving the massive vault door closed. Mechanical locks turned, sealing it into place.

The two wisps were circling her head more and more slowly, dancing lightly. They faded into the air like smoke. "No!" Lyita cried.

Aurelian closed his eyes, and wished his own grandmother love and good travels to wherever she might go. He could swear he felt a loving farewell.

Then he found he had held his eyes closed for too long, for he started to feel faint. Something stopped his fall. He opened his eyes to find he was still upright, and Lyita had put her shoulder under his. "Not yet," she said. "Let's get out of here. Upstairs. We can make it."

He looked wearily the way they had come. "Up those stairs?"

"Yes. Up."

She took off his shirt and wrapped around his wound as best she could. They made it all the way back up the stairs, and then the ladder. She uprighted an overturned chair and sat him down in it, then pulled the improvised bandage off to look at his wound. "We'd better get you to a hospital."

That meant the police could find him. He laughed at such a mundane concern. "I have had some...misunderstandings with the law. Perhaps we can find a veterinarian."

Lyita nodded, not saying anything.

"Thank you," he said at last.

"Don't thank me," she said. "We had our reasons. My parents are free now."

"As is my grandmother." He shook his head. "But you helped her, and you helped me. So I'm thanking you, and there's nothing you can do about it."

In spite of herself, she smiled. Then her expression became thoughtful. She was thinking what to say, and something told him to leave her be until she said it.

"What is it that you want from life, Aurelian?"

"I want to be free," he said without hesitation. "I want a better life."

She found her words. "Sometimes when I hear the dead, I ask them why they stay. It always seems to be because they have regrets. "

"I don't even plan on staying in St. Petersburg."

She laughed. "The best way to not stay, is to let go of your regrets."

"Or to have no regrets at all." He kissed her.

If you enjoyed this story, would you like to leave a review? It can be as easy as selecting the right amount of stars, and leaving just a few words of what you liked.
https://amzn.to/2vv3q3x

ABOUT THE AUTHOR

James Beach is a writer, photographer and recovering musician. He was born and raised in New Jersey, and was once told he was a bad Photoshop superimposition on the East Coast. He successfully escaped and now lives in San Francisco, a perfect locale for exploring his emerging super powers.

For more declassified information, visit
jimbeach.net